WILL'S MAMMOTH

STORY BY
RAFE MARTIN

iLLUSTRATED BY
STEPHEN GAMMELL

The Putnam & Grosset Group

TO A CERTAIN BOULDER OF MY childhood, which TAUGHT me that STONES CAN LIVE.
AND TO MINNIE WOLF... SHE DREAMED DREAMS AND SAW VISIONS.

Pate

TO GRETCHEN SARAH AND BEN.

Stephen

WiLL
LoveD
MAMMOTHS...

...WOOLLY MAMMOTHS.

HIS MOTHER and FATHER HAD TOLD HIM THAT ALL THE MAMMOTHS HAD DISAPPEARED TEN THOUSAND YEARS AGO.

"THERE AREN'T ANY MORE MAMMOTHS, WILL — ANYWHERE."

BUT WILL KNEW THAT THERE WERE.

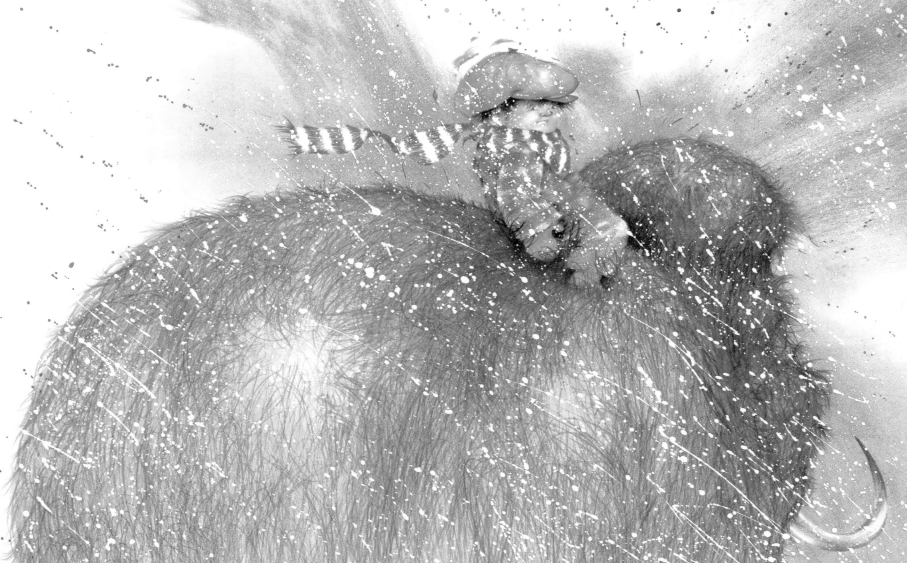

"WHAT DID YOU DO TODAY, WILL?"

"I RODE MY MAMMOTH."